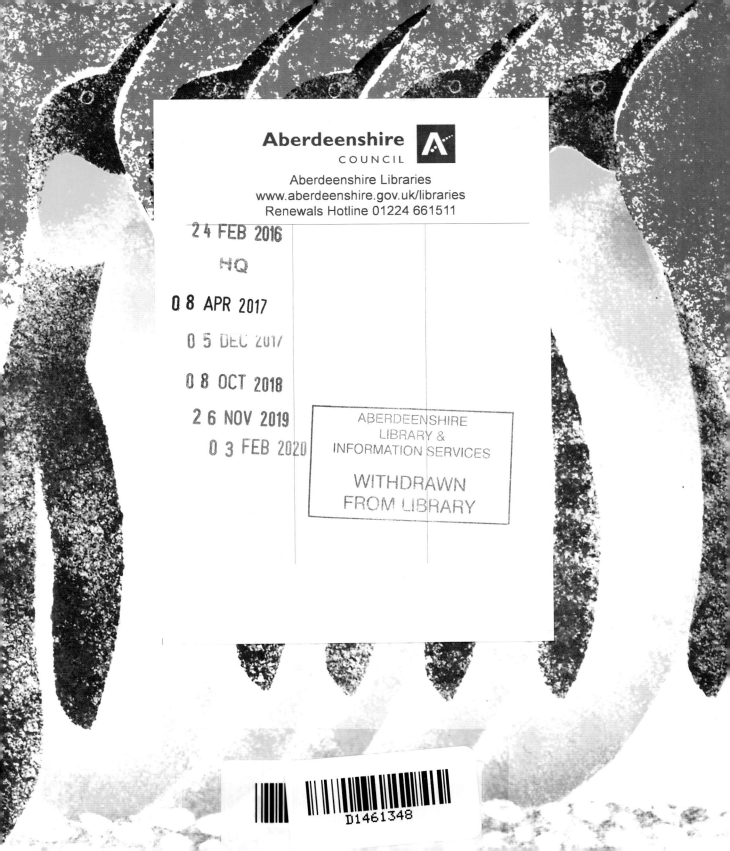

First published in 1962 by Doubleday & Company, Inc., New York

Text © Johanna Johnston, 1962. Illustrations © Leonard Weisgard, 1962. All rights reserved

Reissued in 2015 by the Bodleian Library, Broad Street, Oxford OX1 3BG

www.bodleianshop.co.uk ISBN: 978 1 85124 427 0

Text © The Estate of Johanna Johnston, 2015. Illustrations © The Estate of Leonard Weisgard, 2015. All rights reserved

Printed and bound on FSC paper by Toppan, China.

Penguin's Way

Johanna Johnston Illustrated by Leonard Weisgard

Bodleian Children's Books

FAR, FAR AWAY, near the bottom of the world, there is a secret sea. That is where the emperor penguins swim and fish and play all through the summer.

Then summer ends. One by one, two by two, then by the hundreds, the penguins swim away—toward the lonely lands of snow around the South Pole.

The air grows colder, the water too. At last the penguins come to a great shelf of ice and snow. They leap out of the water and land, *kerflop!* Then they push themselves to their feet with their beaks and wing tips and stand up and look around.

There is no food for them here, no river or pool where they can fish. But they are fat from feasting all summer and they are glad the long journey is done.

They begin to choose partners. Two by two, they stand near each other and sing. They sing strange, echoing songs of love.

Now almost everyone has found a mate. And two by two they wander about on the snow plain or make games out of sliding down little slopes of ice.

But each day the sun is moving closer to the edge of the world and its rays are pale and cold. The nights grow longer and longer. Winter is on its way.

The first blizzard comes. The wind howls in from the South Pole and the air is thick with snow. All the penguins hurry to stand together in a long line. Shoulder locked against shoulder, they make a wall against the storm. The wind beats on their backs, the snow piles up around them, ice crystals freeze on their feathers, but they hold their wall till the storm is over.

Soon there is another blizzard, and another, and another. Soon there is hardly any daylight at all. Still—something wonderful happens. All over the snow plain the penguins begin to sing. The eggs are beginning to arrive.

Each mother penguin holds her egg in a warm hollow just above her feet. She looks down at the egg and sings. The father penguin looks at the egg and he sings too.

But when the egg hatches—what then? What food will
there be for the chick in this cold, dark land? The mother
knows what she must do. Carefully, she lets the egg down
onto the ice and pushes it to the father. Carefully, the
father penguin lifts it onto his feet. The fathers are going
to guard the eggs while the mothers journey to the sea to
find food, and bring it back before the eggs hatch.

The sea is not so near as it was. What once was sea is ice now. The mothers must travel many miles to find open water. But off they go—into the last of the light.

The last of the light, the very last. Then the sun is gone completely, disappeared under the edge of the world, not to shine again for weeks. Real winter has come. The days are as black as the nights and blizzards howl back and forth without stopping. Shoulder to shoulder, the fathers stand on the snow plain, guarding the eggs.

A long time goes by—many days, many nights—
while the wind and the snow and the cold whirl them
down to the deep heart of winter. It is weeks since
the fathers have eaten. They are thin and hungry and
cold. Still they hold their guard. Sometimes they close
their eyes and sleep. Sometimes they just stare into
the storm and wait.

Then … is that a glimmer of light in the sky? The penguins lift their heads and look up. They turn their heads and look toward the sea.

But the glimmer only lasts a few minutes. It is dark again and the blizzard rages on, as before.

Next day the twilight comes again and lasts a little longer. And the next day again. And then at last the fathers see a little black dot coming across the snow. There is another dot and another. The mothers are returning from the sea.

The fathers murmur and sway. And soon the mothers are there. They are fat and glossy from feeding in the sea. And they sing as they hurry to their mates.

Each mother takes back her egg. And the father stands beside her, his hunger and cold forgotten. It is time for the egg to hatch.

The mother stands still as a statue, hearing the shell crack, feeling it move and stir on her feet.

Away off at the edge of the snow plain the light grows brighter. The sun is coming back from below the horizon. There it is. A pale ball at the edge of the world. A long shaft of light glitters across the snow. It only lasts a little while—but long enough, long enough.

Suddenly, the egg-shell cracks open. There is the baby penguin, lying on his mother's feet, a soft little bundle of grey down, his black eyes rimmed with white.

Once again the lonely snow plain echoes with penguin song.

Then the baby stretches up his head and the mother bends her own. And as night comes again she opens her beak to feed him.

The father is very proud of his family. But he cannot forget his own hunger any longer. Besides, winter is far from being over and soon the baby will need more food.

So now, just as the mother left two months ago, the father starts off. All the fathers leave the plain, heading for the sea.

The mothers are too busy to watch them go. The babies are learning to walk and they want to wander everywhere. But cruel birds, the skuas, are waiting. The mothers hurry after the babies whenever they start to waddle away. And still the blizzards are whirling in, day after day after day. Whenever the wind begins to blow, the mothers must round up the babies and make a wall around them with their bodies, for that wind could snatch up a baby and carry him far away.

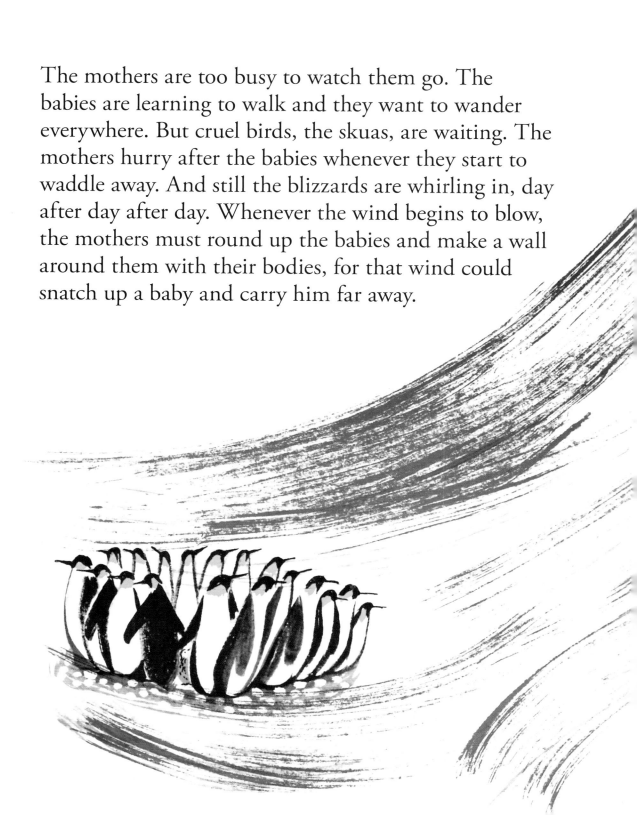

Each day now, the sun stays a little longer and rides a little higher in the sky. But winter is still hard and cold when the fathers come back from the sea. They are plump and shining again, ready to feed the babies.

The babies grow bigger. The fathers feed them till they have given them all the food they brought back. And still the winter holds. And then some strange penguins come walking across the snow.

The penguin chicks do not know them at all, but the mothers and fathers do. They are last year's babies, the yearlings, come back to the snow plain from their own secret sea where they have been spending the winter.

Why have they come—when there is no food for anyone here? They have come because this is where yearlings always come to shed their first feathers and get new, grown-up plumage.

The newcomers stand around shivering, looking thin and tattered. The downy chicks are all ragged now too. And everyone is hungry. When will it really be spring?

All of a sudden there is a far-off *boom*. The ice at the edge of the sea is beginning to break. Spring is coming.

Boom. Boom. Day by day the sounds come closer and that means the open sea is coming closer too.

The penguins chatter and move about, restless with waiting.

There is an enormous *boom.* And the ice cracks right across their own snow plain. A river of dark, cold water is flowing toward the sea. It is spring at last.

The penguins look at each other. And here is a miracle too. The yearlings are wearing fine, new feathers of white and black and midnight blue. And as a sign that they are really grown-up emperors now, they have a golden patch of feathers on either side of their necks.

And look at the chicks. They are babies no more. They too are wearing black and white and midnight blue, just like the others. All that is missing is the golden patch, which they will get next year.

The penguins begin to run back and forth in excitement. Then one of them starts for the river and all of them follow. They walk, they try to run, they flop on the ice and slide. The winter is over, the winter is over—spring has come!

There they are. On the ice at the water's edge. The chicks stare at the water. They have never seen anything like it before but they know they want to dive in. They do not know, as the older ones do, that there can be danger here if sharks swim in from the sea.

One of the penguins makes up his mind. He dives in.
At once all the others dive in too.

It is all right. No sharks are near. There is just the
wonder and the joy of swimming and diving and
gliding in the water which is the penguins' true home.

At last they are all on their way to the sea. The long, long winter is over. Next year they will come back and live through another winter just as dark and cold and terrible, to bring another brood of penguin babies into the world. It is a strange, hard way to live, different from any other bird's. But it is their way, the way of every emperor penguin.

And now, through all the short summer they are free, to swim and fish and play, far, far away, in the heart of their secret sea.